SO-EUK-659

Donated to
SAINT PAUL PUBLIC LIBRARY

WITHDRAWN

TOUR

NEW & SELECTED POEMS

OTHER BOOKS BY PETER SEARS

Secret Writing
Icehouse Beach
The Lady Who Got Me to Say Solong Mom
I Want to Be a Crowd
Bike Run

TOUR

NEW & SELECTED POEMS

PETER SEARS

BREITENBUSH BOOKS
PORTLAND, OREGON

© 1987 by Peter Sears. All rights reserved.

This book, or any part thereof, may not be reproduced by any means, written or mechanical, or be programmed into any electronic retrieval or information storage system, without express written permission from the publisher, except for short passages for purposes of review in television, radio, and periodicals.

First Edition 2 3 4 5 6 7 8 9

Library of Congress Cataloging in Publication Data

Sears, Peter, 1937 —
     Tour.
I. Title
PS3569.E19T6 1987 811'.54 87-5196
ISBN 0-932576-48-6
ISBN 0-932576-49-4 (pbk)

The author and publisher wish to thank the editors of the following publications where many of these poems first appeared.

Antioch Review, Aspen Anthology, Beloit Poetry Journal, Calapooya Collage, Chouteau Review, Chowder Review, Cincinnati Poetry Review, Colorado State Review, Confluence, Dakota Territory, Encore, Hanging Loose, Hellcoal Annual, Iowa Review, KSOR Guide to the Arts, Mother Jones, Ploughshares, Poetry Northwest, Poetry Now, Portland Review, Premiere, Saturday Review, Southern Poetry Review, University of Windsor Review, Upstart; Trask House Press, Raindust Press, Chowder Chapbooks.

The author and publisher are grateful to the National Endowment for the Arts, a Federal Agency, and to Northwest Writers, for their financial assistance in the publication of this book, and to the Metropolitan Arts Commission of Portland, Oregon.

Breitenbush Books are published for James Anderson
by Breitenbush Publications, Box 02137, Portland, OR 97202-0137
Patrick Ames, Editor-in-Chief

Text design by Patrick Ames

Manufactured in the USA

TABLE OF CONTENTS

FAMILY
    2. Bike Run
    3. Icehouse Beach
    4. Grandfather and the Rabbit
    5. Judy Margolis, Be Still Impossibly Lovely
    6. By the Pond
    7. The Moonlight Is Deep and Long
    8. Goodbye
    9. Skimpy
  10. A Place for Four-Letter Words
  11. Brother
  12. To a Young Woman Considering Suicide
  13. The Whooping Crane
  14. The Family Who Went to Sleep
  15. A Story
  16. To Our Daughter of Three Months

VOICES
  18. Dear Mr. Sears
  19. The Lady Who Got Me to Say Solong Mom
  20. The Man in the Photo with His Corn
  21. Escape from East Berlin
  22. How Old Tom Swank Got the Name Mammoth
  23. You've Got a Right
  24. Deep Vague
  25. Fogbank
  26. Vineyard Gazette, Classified
  27. I'll Give You Fall and Winter
  28. The Road
  29. Nights Are My Deep Oceans
  30. The Drinker
  32. Rain
  33. Openers
  34. A Voice Collapsing

DARK DREAMS
- 36. Burntown
- 37. Trip Up the Dark
- 38. Dream of the Moon Tree Girl
- 39. The Tablecloth Explanation
- 40. The Man in My Dreams
- 41. Oil Slick
- 42. We Are Tired of Talk of New Safety Measures
- 43. Who Can Love a Man Who Can't Sleep?
- 44. The Man with Loose Skin
- 45. Vulture
- 46. The Deep Lover of My Barbara Is Silence
- 47. It's in the Eyes
- 48. He Comes as Wind
- 49. We Went Dreaming the Valley of the Black Soil
- 50. Ditch
- 51. The Darkness

MOVING AROUND
- 54. Tour
- 55. I First Practiced Picking Up Small Things
- 56. Bridgeport
- 57. Bargain
- 58. Truck
- 59. American Hero: A Poem Made into a Movie
- 60. Chicago
- 61. Moon Gliding
- 62. Universe of Kansas
- 63. Dodo Birds
- 64. Lip's Lounge
- 65. King Tongue
- 66. A Night and Morning First Time Drive to Portland
- 67. Hands
- 68. Bottoming Out
- 69. The Lady with the Laughing Gas Lover
- 70. Demolition of Grand Central Station

FACING UP

72. The Season We Haven't Named
73. Silence
74. Turning to Women
76. The Man Who Reads Your Whole Library
77. Horse Head Swamp
78. The Guard
80. Night Beach
81. Unwinding
82. Time of Mud
83. Encounter
84. The Sludge
85. Night Golf
86. At the Coast
87. Request
88. Slack Tide
89. Skylight of a Well Lit Brain
90. Looking Ahead
91. Coming Apart Nicely in the Fifth Street Market

for Rivers Sears

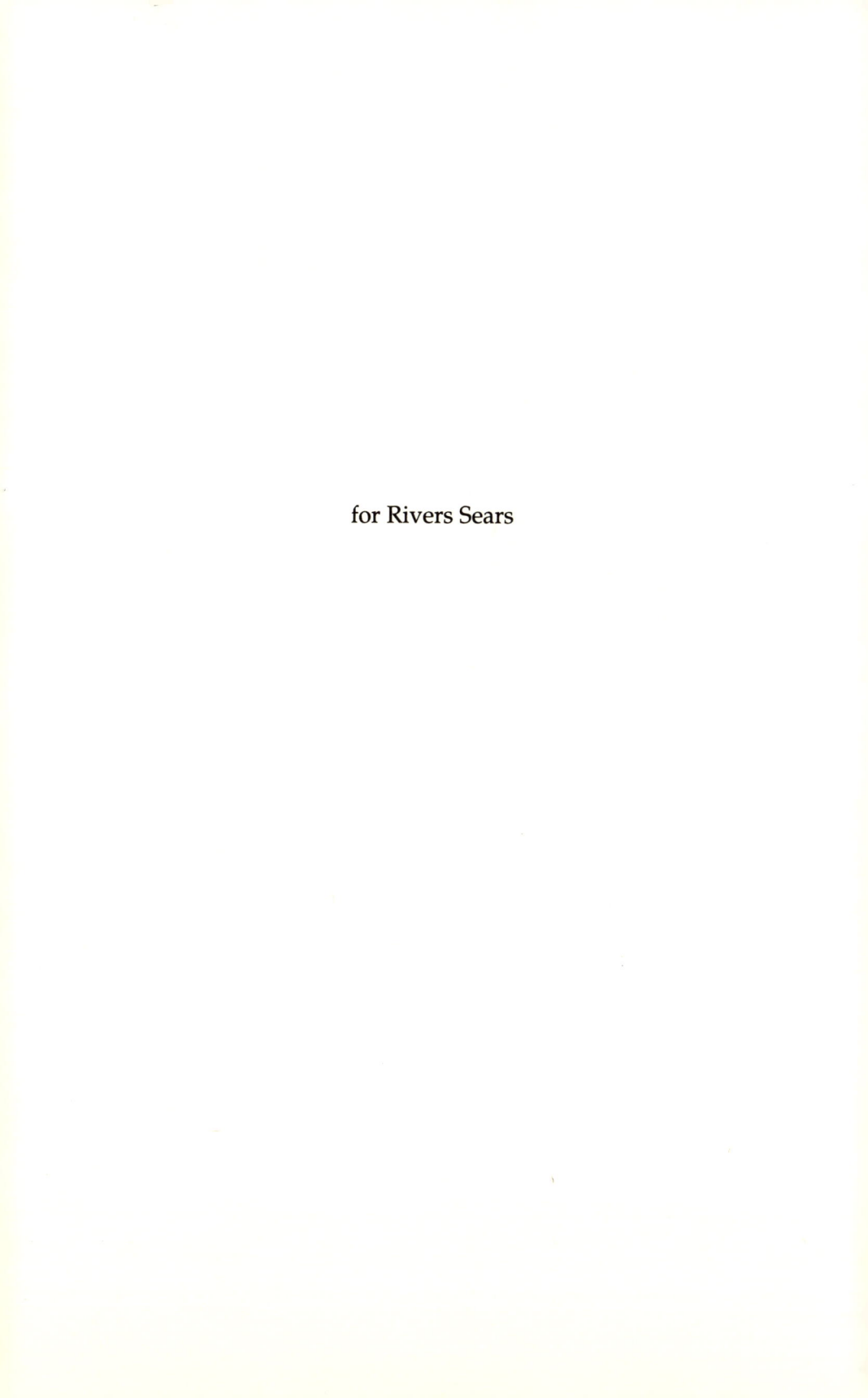

FAMILY

Bike Run

Old summers would begin
wearing down the path again, the bike run
that slit the hip-high field into long triangles.

Hit the start hard and standing, jump
the rock gap, the gully, feet up
for puddles in the middle.

Slick along the packed sand
and streak out the other end
leaning on the sky,

And the breathless one inside you,
who wants to sleep in high grass,
tell him there is a path through,

That you made the path through.
Show him, tell him again;
make him shout, I believe you.

Icehouse Beach

My father swims by again I can see
his mouth come over open sideways
his eye come up the other is always
under I see the eye always under
see it behind my eyes and I run
for him on the beach waving the way
his arms go in his long swimming

mother goes into the water waits
floating on her back she kicks out
splashes him he goes by one arm
up she's laughing she's spinning
up that water will she really break
into his swimming she knows how far
he and the ocean go away how his work
is like the water it floats in our
house we're always getting ready

hurry your father's coming I know
how she throws back her hair
when she has waited through his work
she does little paddles with her
hands she's afraid he'll think
someday she's just a person living
here I can't go away his head
just hair and an eye there

the eye I see is always under
she's wrong she looks for things
to be afraid of when there's just us
in the rooms watching the sun come
low making up things we've done
to tell him something when he
takes us both and breathes out

Grandfather and the Rabbit

Upstate, in a town with brown benches
and stores with houses on top of them,
we stopped the car along a high stone sidewalk
and father led us to Grandfather's church,
planks, thick with paint, a bird's nest
by the door, official man in the door.
He leaned a little like a tree
and smiled so fast his eye blinked.

The church went straight to the altar.
Rows went out like bones of big wings.
I felt the organ playing through the floor,
like the towns, driving up,
getting lower and farther away.

Most towns up here went away years ago,
father said, when the textile mills
moved south. I didn't understand. I thought
Grandfather died softly like snow.

Father spun the wheel
to miss a rabbit crushed on the road.
He tried to blend his swerve into a turn,
and mother mentioned flowers and how well
they plow the roads up here. Lines
in her face were trees across a cloud.
I puffed up my window and drew eyes.

I know how rabbits die on roads
but Grandfather in this place,
what happened to his thud step?
It's out there. I want to be out there.

We were standing in the pew. I stepped on
my shined shoes. Mother gave me her hand.
I let it go away.

Judy Margolis, Be Still Impossibly Lovely

Years I watched your house from right field,
Big Farn unloading fungo shots at your yard,
daring us shrimps to slither up. I was ten,
you went to college then. That last spring,

Batting against Farn, hating the heavy bats,
choking up and still I was the easy whiff;
hell, Farn threw so hard the ball went egg,
said if I didn't swing he'd dust me off.

Fat-ass Farn uncorks again. I frazzle blind,
swing early — thud waved around second, Farn
staring at your house. Your father lets me in,
leads me up to the broken window, the ball,

You, your room. I kneel, pick up broken glass.
"That's dumb, boy. Judy, get a broom. And boy,
find yourself another field. You're too big."
I had never been too big. Your dress, I breathed

It in. You left, your father left, and how could
you let your little sister say "oh the pounding
I would get" and you forgot some glass over
here and over here, even asked me if I hit it
and why was I so small. Judy, where is she?

By the Pond

Barefoot and wrapped in her daughter's
wrinkled khaki raincoat she hesitates
by the pond. The wind that snapped all afternoon,
wheezing through her bungalow,
is down. Foam has bundled in the grasses.
She takes a tall grass in her toes,
waves it, and lets go.
Sound from across the pond
slides over to her.
The pond turns dusk pink.
The shade lies like oil
and will die before dark.
She rolls her feet in the water
and pulls the raincoat around her.

The Moonlight Is Deep and Long

after a poem by William Carlos Williams

We have stayed out too long and still
we haven't picked enough fruit.
Our parents, we'll catch hell;
but if we can pick enough,
maybe they will let us out
tomorrow night. Let's bring back
baskets of pears! The heat, I said,
is why I lagged behind today.
Anyway, stars are easier
than all those people.
Your eyes shine so. The wind
is cool enough to walk with.
Look at this basket of pears,
cool skins of the moon's attention.
Baskets and baskets of pears!
Look at you in the moonlight.

Goodbye

Have we really said goodbye
and now, and now? We look around
as if someone is coming.
What you say next
will startle me. I wish
we could fall into the hour
and laugh ourselves through.

Skimpy

I'm the older brother, cookie of the clan
the family said, but yawning made me dizzy,
sneezing scared me. I'd sit down.
I learned to brood, practiced on dogs
and bathroom mirrors, made my room
into a car, made up sounds
for everywhere, but like the brooding
I had nothing around to go anywhere.
Now I say, if you shut up too long
your breath gets rancid.

I made it go: health foods,
pep them up with a swat of ketchup.
Jog a lot. Feel red as a fire engine,
feel in one place at a time.
Give it right back to the bathroom mirror.
And my own business too. Toys of Joy.
So tell the family I look myself in the eye,
that I have friends to call from airports.
Tell them — tell them anything
but make them think of me.

A Place for Four-Letter Words

I had it all wrong from the start
about four-letter words. I thought
they were big words with four letters.

I thought about being wrong.
I kept it quiet, cobweb quiet,
like our house, even our garage.

All but the shed where I kept
my bike. I looked for a place
to hear the words, all of them.

Before someone tried to tell me
where this one belonged and that
one didn't. Leaning streamlined

Over the handlebars, I heard them
in the tire's lick and spin. Faster,
tearing all out down a hill, hunched

Under the wind, blinking at the rain,
I yelled every four-letter word I knew,
yelled them until they were as real

As the hill, yelled them until I
broke them in the spokes and they were
just words spinning in the spokes.

Brother

You are only two years into your city.
Come back to nights when wind paws trees
and we have to talk to fall asleep.
Back into late afternoons
when the light strokes the gray pond
and the sun rocks long-haired in the reeds.

We ease in, sputtering the chill.
The sandy bottom loosens, comes smoking
to the surface, and we're under and rolling
in colors sliding like oil on water.

How still we float to let the wind
fall asleep on the pond,
then wake the wind, feel it brush
our backs like short fur. Tell me what burns
when the wind breaks in on the sun,
there, where the reeds lean away.

To a Young Woman Considering Suicide

When everything you touch you've already touched,
you can't sleep, can't eat, can't even
remember when you could, you go on living;

When everywhere you are you want to leave,
it's so stupid, stupid not to go down
with the sun, down with leaves spiraling,

Down with the duck pulled under
by the muskrat, waves, they don't roll in,
they roll down and die — even now, you go on living.

Would you help me with my plant?
See, it's not doing well at all, and out
there in the snow my friend's car is stuck.

He needs a hand, what do you think? —
More light? A bigger pot? And what do I say
to my child, to your child someday,
if she goes out, as you have, under the long shadow?

The Whooping Crane

Do you remember hearing about the Whooping Crane
being assigned to a flock of Sandhill Cranes?
Do you ever wonder how it is doing?
How can we tell? The crane may die of boredom
or strangeness. Please, someone, try to say;
and don't say 'The Whooper,' not even for fun.
Just the Whooping Crane and how it's to find a mate.
We saw it, my wife and I, in New Mexico.
Sandhill Cranes fly right over town we heard.
We watched for them. Perhaps they crossed at night,
on to Bosque del Apache, or to the smaller reserve
at Bernardo. We drove to Bernardo
and saw them gracious in a field,
the Sandhill Cranes and one Whooping Crane.
I tried to see them all, tried to breathe slowly
into gazing into the field. Again and again
the field narrowed to the one crane.
I want to know how the Whooping Crane is doing.

The Family Who Went to Sleep

When the Krenshaws went to sleep, my parents said, "What do you mean? They can't do that!" and looked at me. "All I know is what I hear at school. The father lost his job. They are going to sleep for a year." "Ridiculous!" my father boomed and the fish in the aquarium stopped. "Don't set foot on their property." I didn't say I walk home that way from school, that my friends are pretty mean to the Krenshaw kids, who won't fight, won't even talk. The one in my class won't share my big lunch. I wonder what it would be like going into homeroom a year behind.

What if I had to? What if my father lost his job and we had to sleep until he got another? How would he do it? I'd stay awake with him and sneak to the Krenshaws. They might still be asleep. What if no one is around to talk to? — just a few people waking up sometimes? It wouldn't work. Things would stop, fall apart. Enough people would have to stay awake to take care of the people asleep. When a family woke up, there would have to be enough food. I want to be awake when the Krenshaws wake up.

A Story

When his father came to his room,
the boy made himself so small
his father couldn't see him,
and when his father wouldn't leave,
the boy made himself so large
his father couldn't see his head,
and the boy had to hold his breath
not to crush him, backing out.

When his father visited his teacher,
the boy so stretched himself through time
his father couldn't tell who the teacher
was talking about and became furious.
When he could again think of his son,
the boy vanished, even as an idea.

When his father felt love for his son
without thinking it and rushed
to see if his son was all right,
the boy could only imagine
his father's love and could only
imagine the son his father loved
and vanished, even to himself.

To Our Daughter of Three Months

Be wise I tell myself: say nothing grand
with the righteous kicker of should.
Trust yourself and your ease will be
a climate your daughter can trust.
But I'm so fast. Flick, I am father
the double man. My years rise in a wave
and span my blood beating out beyond
my own. Flick, my life beats double time.

So be wise I say: say nothing until you ask.
What does your understanding need beyond
its own blue growing? I want most for you
time to follow your own becoming.

And when you like your own being,
you will love more fully than I love you now,
already, by the blood and for the chance
you give me to care for you. Too soon though
I will have to give up this caring for you.
How? By learning to love you openly
like a cloud flowing across water.

VOICES

Dear Mr. Sears

Dear Mr. Sears,
　I want to write you about your poem about the frog. I love frogs. I raised one once. My mother made me stop kissing it. I like your poem.
　　　　　　　Yours sincerely,
　　　　　　　Mrs. X

Dear Mrs. X,
　Thank you. Writers appreciate a personal response — what else is there? Where is Brule, Nebraska? And where did you see the poem? I don't recall it. Really. Which makes me feel pretty silly. Please sign your name. It's good of you to write.
　　　　　　　Yours truly,
　　　　　　　Peter Sears

Dear Mr. Sears,
　It must be strange not to recall the poem. That's all right. Here are the last two lines, my favorites —
　　I roll the frog over on its back
　　and tickle him under his little chin sack.
　　　　　　　Sincerely yours,
　　　　　　　Mrs. X

Dear Person,
　I can see why you like the poem, but I didn't think frogs stayed put that long. Anyway, I can't take credit for the poem. And yes, it is strange.
　　　　　　　Yours,
　　　　　　　Peter Sears

Dear Mr Sears,
　The poem is 'My Friend the Frog' published in the third grade paper. The rest of the poem is blurred by dirt and leaves.
　　　　　　　Yours,
　　　　　　　a friend

The Lady Who Got Me to Say Solong Mom

Somewhere along the lettuce I nudge a lady who says
Amazing how you resemble my daughter! At the yogurt
we meet again. Would you say Solong Mom for an old
woman who misses her daughter?...Why not, for a lady
daffy in loneliness, Solong Mom. I end up behind her
at the checkout line. The guy rings up my lettuce,
yogurt and yam and says $43.16...What! You're nuts!
...Your mother says the checkbook's in your purse.

My mother! She's not my mother. Out the door I shoot,
scan the parking lot. She's loading up the backseat,
the frontseat. Hey, get back in and pay! She hips me,
we grapple. She's strong, then she's sad and weak,
standing there, staring around. The cart rolls off,
a bag dumps. We grab at each other. This is crazy.
She tilts her head, I tilt mine. Smack! She gets me
one good. I clout her. Get back in there and pay!

Whoopee! she yelps and gallops around me whoopeeing,
swinging her purse, and pops me on the nose. I tackle
her, grab a skinny leg, drag her across the lot like
an old hose, through the whooshing door, squiggling,
kicking. The manager hollers, What's going on?...
This lady just tried to rob me by pretending she's
my mother. That's right. Ask the checkout guy. $43.16
for my lettuce, yogurt and yam...Is that true, ma'am?

I don't have a daughter, I don't have a son. Cats
and a parakeet named Oswald who's deaf. He loves
the three-way lightbulbs I lift from Woolworth's.
My old kook roommate babbles about being a princess.
It's enough to make you want to flush your head. This
girl is the daughter I really want. I want to ask her
back for dinner. I feel a lot better now. Thanks.

The Man in the Photo with His Corn

— for Floyd Bahmler

Had my picture taken with my corn,
July 4th, see, right up to my chest,
and when I stretch the leaves
they come like kisses to my cheeks.

Then in August come tassels
and ears right out with them.
Next pollen and silk
from the ears. Yellow pollen

From the tassels falls on cornsilk.
The kernel forms. It's worth long
days when the sky rolls deep dark like
a sick whale. Everyone's got the moans.

Why, I can moan louder longer than
a Chinese opera, but that's better
than drinking my way down to eating
paper. That's why the picture.

I wanted that picture standing in
my corn, so I can be good as a goat
on ledges late at night.
I can pull it out, look at it,

Remember smoking cornsilk rolled
in shoebox paper like we did as kids,
buy a round of drinks and think
about corn brimming in the cribs.

Escape from East Berlin

The Berlin Wall went through our heads.
Fed by day, by our staying in the East,
we drank it out at night. Our heads got
soft as beer. We toasted our escape plan,
the only place the Vopos hadn't walled,
where the river widens and searchlights
swing like waltzers. A guard could fire
and load again. A man could have a smoke.
This worst chance made our chances fair.

We swam the river and won't leave this bank.
Others will hear how we went and wonder
why not and plan. Before they can move,
police will hear and alert the authorities,
who will alert the border guards, and they
will alert the river, the dogs, the night.
There in the high grass on the east side,
is that a rock that tries to be the moon?
A face? A searchlight rolls the grass.

Stay down. Flush your stomach to the grass.
Count the black time between each beam.
Your heart jacks up the count. The brain
blows black and yellow. Count it hard
again. You've got to bet. Go, push off
from the cold sand lip. Hold your kick
until you're under; then kick, pull down
through the dark. Don't nick the top
until the beat is nailing down your throat.

How Old Tom Swank
Got the Name Mammoth

I'm so poor I only have ashtrays on weekends
and I'm not known for doing anyone any good
or any better but I like the name I came by
the blizzard night when double shots dropped
me in snowbanks drifting McClancey's Grocery

so when a blizzard comes people say I'm off
to do the mammoth which isn't even a snow
angel but I think into the sky and wonder
what in us lasts and if that thing would
let us finally sleep if it had its own way

You've Got a Right

I heard you were coming my way,
saying funny things to people and not explaining,
going around a little deaf. You've got a right.
I figured we should meet.
We'll take your car, it's got brakes.

I know about the laundromat,
your climbing in, singing warm spin warm spin.
You'd been mush.

And that goof dog Hairball,
I hear you run with him at night.
You like the lake, the moon, the creamy ice,
and riding garbage cans down the banks.

You need a girl.
I know one who curls around her terrarium
fingering trails.
She loves a carwash,
the sprayers and those crazy rubber suckers.

You'll be the one.
She reads too much now
and who says you can't hold a job, come on back.
She'll rush your cellar up your stairs.

Deep Vague

You look at me and your eyes keep going.
Where? You are weather at the coast
I'm driving to and guessing.
I'm never right. You'll be late
and apologize me crazy. When I insist
you stop, you'll bounce me around
for lying nicely. Whatever I do
I'm trying too hard. You seem to want
what you're always removing things from.
Why do I always want to thank you
for something you haven't done?
You're the cat you feed that won't come in.

Fogbank

I am Fogbank. Born casual and drifty
I added leaping hedges and grinning,
if caught, with an electric face.
Why talk when you can stay gray
as your name? Rise, Fogbank, shuffle

The school steps, the job steps, loft
your dream flesh over mobile homes,
perch on the treeline of a deep estate,
soothe girls iceteaing on the terrace,
bored as cardboard, eager as pebbles
in the brook. Stretch out in the brook,

Dangle while the mother of all money
and things with names affirms: "I wish
more young men could act this way."
I know who to thank, but save it until
after dinner, when brandy has my tongue.

Old Whiffleball, I'm heading upwind,
frisky, and shadowbox. I am my own
prune's pit. I've never had an arm die
or an eye, nothing that tests the grain.
I've pickled long enough. Step into the
nightmare knucklers, the breaking stuff.

Vineyard Gazette, Classified

Would the good person who
called me last September
to say I left my Venetian
turquoise enamel and gold
compact at his house please
call again. Beth 693-9707

I'll Give You Fall and Winter

Why didn't you stay in the windy fall
where you left me
to flap around my hard house?

Why didn't you stay in the dense winter
where you held me
tight as ice against my memory of you?

And now spring too, why? Spring's
not like you. Buds, what can I do
against what they lift in me?

The Road

Knock on the door. Two men and two men, they go to the corners of the room. WE SAW YOUR FLOWER BY YOUR DOOR. Yes, it came up yesterday. DID YOU PLANT MANY? I didn't plant any. WOULD YOU LIKE TO? WOULD YOU LIKE TO CHANGE? I'm thinking maybe a church group. I have a dollar, a quarter. YOU WERE OUT ON THE ROAD LAST NIGHT, WALKING BACK AND FORTH. WERE YOU TROUBLED? WE WILL GO IF YOU WANT US TO. You seem to be getting to the point. HOW DO YOU FEEL NOW? I might plant some flowers. DO YOU HAVE OTHER QUESTIONS? No. DID YOU HAVE ANY LAST NIGHT, OUT ON THE ROAD? This is silly walking around the room, shaking hands. DID YOU LIKE THE FACT THAT THE BIRDS ARE ASLEEP? Huh, I didn't notice. PERHAPS WE CAN TALK ANOTHER TIME. I like the light.

Nights Are My Deep Oceans

She combs her hair and humming
dreams each long stroke off to trees
cooling in the summer night, lifting
and swaying to each long stroke
she stretches to summer night trees.

She laughs as her hair lifts
to her bidding, as each turn
in the trees draws in her humming,
and she hears someone say he would
change nothing of wind in night trees

and surely nothing she favors,
but he could change her, could give her
spring, give her summer of only days
— ah but nights she says,
nights are my deep oceans.

The Drinker

Five Saturdays now my neighbor
makes the package store
by nine o'clock, then the six

blocks back with a bag of beer
and sits in his sling chair
that has been his backyard for the spring.

When he's empty, it's back for more.
Even thunder
only lifts his forehead off his chin.

At night too he's out there.
That's his affair, but what if later
some long night

a knocking — I get up, go to the door,
turn on the light, and he appears?
Let him in I guess

and say whatever keeps me talking.
But he won't come here,
I know that, and I'm not going over there.

So what's the fuss?
Maybe he's on it, trying to figure
out what really matters.

What do I know? —
I'm nicer to my job, my car,
than I am to my heart.

But drop everything
to concentrate on what I care
about? That's too vague. I'm happier

on the move. Still, it can't hurt
to take a chair
out back for an hour or so.

Rain

There is more than one rain. There is rain
that drones, how far and deep I don't know,
and rain that rattles leaves and gutters,

chattering windows. Yes, and another, wind rain,
think of wind rain, how it flattens and angles.
See, there are three rains. And what of the one

we don't hear or see, the one the brain
doesn't know — do you know this rain? Yes,
and I know another, the rain I smell

flowing the sky and I look to birds and flowers
tuning, and the air, how it slows. There are more,
listen, listen! Do you hear the deep rain?

Openers

So you want to go up to someone and say
Scappoose! and you'd like to go over
to anyone and bow and bow and rising say
Nehalem. Please don't. Make up as many

openers as you want, as many as the
years passing over oceans, but don't
say them. It's foolish. That's OK
but it's helpless. Really. Sorry.

Scappoose! See? What's someone to say?
Nothing. Except Scappoose back.
Then what? See what I mean?
So you want to go up to someone

and right on by, keeping the lid on
What do you think is an original pet?
or, Will we be known centuries from now
as the people with hair? See how silly

it is? You're laughing! That proves it.
So just Scappoose yourself and have
a good laugh. Let those tears
swamp your nose. Just like that, yes.

Come on, you old Scappoose, hold on
to me. Good. Now let's bow. You can
do it. Nehalem. Off the second bow.
Nehalem. Good. Again. Nehalem.

A Voice Collapsing

OK OK, so we look into dark,
out there, inside, sure we're alone.
So what, we got air, we got water and sod,
and look, nimble fingers! Yet we long
to take all time, death, and fear
and give it a mind. That way we're a plan
for ourselves to unravel. We rise
through our minds to see how we matter.
O we lift our light to a crazy bright!

Have you felt this real, felt it so right
it won't go away, then when you need it,
gone, it's gone? Take heart! Make up
a question and answer for something you
like. Babies? Sure. What do they dream?
And how did it feel the first time
Earth curved over for you, a ball
like your head spinning through what?

Are you getting a feel? What opens the day?
You're swinging your arms. They are long.
Would you like my hat? It's on backwards
for fun. You're standing close. Do you
mind my voice? You won't find a thing
over there. I'm hungry. Sometimes I get
the hammers. We may have to wing it,
we may have to quit. You're not as short
as I thought. Please keep the hat.

DARK DREAMS

Burntown

Our town is on fire underground.
A coal vein caught and burned
through months ago. Dynamite
backfired, blew the burn deeper.
The coal that roots this land
could blaze before anyone could
douse it. Signs coming into town
are painted HELLTOWN, BURNTOWN.
Yesterday the McCullough kid
about fell through. The ground
broke, the kid said, and fizzed.
City reporters jumped on it,
said it could happen anywhere.
Not true. We know the places
that could burst. We know the
hissing that comes before. Are
we so dumb, all of us together,
we can't stop a fire underground?
You think harder when you can't
work and have to hear the same
joke about frying eggs over
vents in the ground. The steam.
The glow. Sidewalks are pink
all night. Streetlights
are pink. We replace curtains
with thick drapes. They all
look pink. Someone will break,
scream through the pink night,
burn this town to the ground.

Trip Up the Dark

He cut a clearing out of the woods
and tried to learn how to spit in the eye
of eyes that come on and go off in the woods.

In came the dark. It lifted the wind.
A sound jumped the night, almost bit it in two
and was gone before he thought of a name.

He listened for steps across wooden boards.
He thought through the house, checked both doors.
What stopped out there? Come now if you're coming.

You sleep all day, creep all night kind,
you wait for the weak, you kill and you eat;
then you stretch and yawn and wait for its kin.

You would circle the wind to kill again!
But nothing and nothing and nothing at dawn.
He drove his lost sleep into his ax.

He drove the whole day into tearing out stumps
and began to learn how to spit in the eye
of things that come on and go off in the woods.

Dream of the Moon Tree Girl

He falls asleep into his own movie, gathers
wet strips of film, carries them to a tree
and drapes them on a branch. He raises one
to the moon. A girl moves in the frame

As the frame moves in his hand and her hair
goes into the tree where the tree
meets the moon. He hears her hair entwining
in the moon on the tree. She calls him

To lift the dark from her hair. He leaps
for a branch, grappling in the light
he keeps moving, batters the tree,
drives it into his hands and lifts them

Ringing to the moon. The tree twists,
the moon slices at it. He stumbles
like a tree dragging roots. She takes him
pounding in tighter and tighter.

The Tablecloth Explanation

It's all because the round man with the pumpkin neck
was teaching no one in particular macadam composition,
and because a lady giggled like dry fire when the

bartender who liked lighting his lighter and looking
at it said a fellow wanted to be a vampire to get
the inside story but he had bad knees from football,

so he talked ladies into sponsoring a blood bank
and they all lounged in the blood bank lobby in
cracked leather chairs and sweep-around sunglasses,

gurgling, snoozing, bloated as ticks. Meanwhile,
I was sharpening my fork under the table,
under my napkin, humming over the ominous grating,

figuring one turn in the air maybe two, depending,
depending on the balance of the fork.
Thud a couple in the walls about ear high

to keep them at bay, but they charged me with chairs
and water-pitcher grenades and tied me up in these
tablecloths. I was badly outnumbered, officer.

The Man in My Dreams

There's a man in my dreams I try to avoid.
He has a suitcase of skins. He zippers
himself into one, then another,

in bathrooms on trains, takes over
everyone I dream, even you, whom I envy
and plead with to take me over entirely,

to end this supposing someone else.
Do you understand? I mean, do you feel
at times like a motel? Do you wake in

the night to the sounds of birds feeding?
I'm afraid of who I am. I dream
another, you, to believe in me.

Oil Slick

A tanker split. The slick came huge
like a mile of jellyfish oozing in.
Streams bubbled, foamed like detergent.
Eyes smarted. Don't rub them we said,
but it made you dizzy if you didn't.
Headaches, coughing, ringing ears,
like the flu, except old people
fainted, grass crinkled, and birds
flew into walls. In the morning
snow that itched, stung, and forced us down.
We fled, going for good air under bushes,
scratching the ground loose, putting
our mouths in and inhaling. We kept
our eyes closed until our heads
straightened out, then went on,
rubbing from our eyes that something
like insecticide. We found this cave.
We didn't know.

We Are Tired of Talk of
New Safety Measures

Freights haul deadly gas right by our school.
The track is in disrepair.
One is sure to derail,

Buckle and roll.
How can they ignore
that freights haul deadly gas right by our school,

By the playground where boys and girls
wave to the engineer?
One is sure to derail.

If one tanker car spills
anywhere along this line — Oh Lord,
freights haul deadly gas right by our school!

We plead with the track inspector. We call
the Health Office. We tell our School Board
one is sure to derail.

What else can we do? — Pray, yell,
stumble away? What good then is it to care
that freights haul deadly gas right by our school?
One is sure to derail.

Who Can Love a Man Who Can't Sleep?

The belly of the horse we rode bloated.
We walked alongside. The swelling eased.
We rode again, slowly. The horse rolled,
died underneath us and when we went down
the way out was all the way down.

Starlings single out a tree and pack it.
The clattering branches try to let go.
The birds lift, black leaves, black leaves.

Lake ice, so thin it breathes,
presses to the shore. Long sheets
crackle on the bank. The ice gives itself away.

I sit by the body of the horse,
sit very hard, wrap my arms around my knees
and try to hug it in,
but nights are gristle. Spit them out in bed.
Who can love a man who can't sleep?

Weeks pack like gutter leaves I scrub out
with my teeth. I hear teeth.
Everywhere my head has teeth.

The Man with Loose Skin

I wrinkle all over. I try to smoothe
and move slowly. Walking bobbles me.
My bones are fog. I'm always moist.
I should leave. That's dumb,
I know. Here is always here
and people get used to you.
You can keep away without leaving.
It was harder when I was young.
I was afraid. As I grew up
I went way inside and got smaller.
My friends jabber they are my friends
and I must learn to forget.
I want to erupt, bury friends,
catch them as they are catching a breath
to babble on. More than revenge
I want a reason for my loose skin.

Vulture

Excuse me Miss, but why do you stand so long
by this painting? Just because it's gilt framed
that doesn't make it a masterpiece. I know,
the vulture dismembering the rabbit is sad,
I suppose, but really it's funk sensationalism,
and I can see by your lovely paisley dress
that you have good taste. Is this for research?
Then note the theatrical light, the grand scale,
and how divorced the forest background is
from this macabre foreground scene.
Why then, may I ask, do you stand so close
and stare at the corner of the forest?

Oh, it's the girl in the back, in the white gown,
snarled and shrouded in the thorny matted foliage.
She seems transfixed, captured for an instant
by the horror of the rabbit's death,
and her face is like the face of the rabbit.
Rather morbid, but weird, yes, I see what
you mean: how can she just stand there and
scratch her back against the wet black bark?
Good point. How can she stand
before that apparition? — You know,
she seems almost to be purring.
I fancy I hear her purring and I feel
the beat of the vulture's wings as she purrs.
Yes, just like that, good for you!

The Deep Lover of My Barbara Is Silence

She tells me we are the love
she dreamed young when she gave
birds names. But when she fades

back, back, back, she's his.
He rolls her shoulders up
her neck. He dangles her lips

heavy off her mouth. I place
her feet in a bowl of water,
I take her hands and whisper

to gestures. I kiss her hands
and ask them to say hello
to her heart for me. I tell

her that her cat sinks
back into high grass like
a stream reversing. Come see,

let's go outside, it's lovely!
The names of flowers sing.
I'll name each flower you are to me!

It's in the Eyes

What do cannibals do first when they catch you?
Lick. They want to know what to expect. Now
if they back off, surprise them: offer one
a lick. Stare. Tempt him to doubt his tongue.
Eyeball one goon over to you and with scorn
blistering indicate to him that the water has
been left unattended. — Stoke it, stoke it,
you toady! And wood, get wood! — Shame them
and when they get pots, utensils, condiments
and their breast-beating statues, take charge.

The ones gathering straw, kick their butts,
lick at them, laugh. — More straw, boobies!
Decadent, you guys are decadent. Hell, you've
got no taste. — Next, the tasty combinations
gambit. Grab yams, line them along your leg,
motion a fire underneath and bite your leg.
Lick the blood long. Look up and laugh, laugh!
Then take carrots, apples and oil, mash them
coated up your arms, and wink the nearest goon
to come on up and sniff. Your tongue tells him
when he may lick, and just as they grow still

Bite down, down, the blood, yick, the bite
curdling to puke, but stare them down, this
is crucial. Then let them laugh and make up
their own combinations: smearing an arm, a leg,
yelling, running around, and when they get
an audience, biting deep, deep. Ignore them.
Select quieter ones and finger in the sand
precise designs of other dishes.

He Comes as Wind

What if He comes disguised as air?
What if He wants to wander, to feel around
in what He's done, and comes as wind?

The people who bought a new something to wear,
are they to line up and be quiet?
The milling around, the short tempers,

And someone goading us on:
Look how the grass leans,
how the twigs are split open wide!

Yet the chill, just in the idea,
like the man there, is he shuddering
or is our anticipation quivering?

The wind may just be wind.
Then how do we appear to Him?
Listen, the wind is on us and gone.

And what if He comes without disguise?
Can we be with Him when He's here?
Does He let us imagine ourselves,

His way of kidding us along,
so that He can invent Himself again
in the notion: He comes as wind?

We Went Dreaming the Valley of the Black Soil

We went dreaming the valley of the black soil,
across land we could have stayed in,
out there, always out there;
nights fell into each other, walking
was the only place to sleep.
We ended here where you're digging
but were gone before our bodies
opened to bones and our bones blazed,
even as sand they blazed — what can you do?
Down on your knees you dig and scrape
and clank. There, a busted tool
we threw away. You sigh over it.
You fondle worked rocks. You finger
everything, but your heart, could you heave
it up hill after hill, days of talking
to your feet, of walking so you won't
lie down; heave your heart
until the land below greens
and you eat out of your eyes,
then pounce on the valley of the black soil,
eat it alive? Ha! you've never had to dream.

Ditch

I drive my work home
and drink it into dinner.
You pretend I'm home,
on time, and everything
is fine. You warm up
dinner with children news.
You're an improv salesplan
I maneuvered and pulled
out of. You're a cut
I let infect, a ditch
I bring you from
places I hate all day
and crush and pave.
Your vacant look
opens everywhere.
We have moved
everywhere. If only
I could hold civil
for this whole
evening, then
beat my gut clean
before the next.

The Darkness

Say you are out for a walk
and somewhere through trees
you walk out of everything in your head

or off by a window in thought
and what you look out to
a crease of trees perhaps you don't see at all
but what you are thinking there in the trees

as you open like this through a window
or walk and walk into a gazing
then say darkness falls

darkness farther back than the cave you felt into
farther back than violence to animals

darkness farther back than water you dove into
hands in front of your face
to feel your way down and know
this darkness did not begin did not gather

then something backing off it seems as you come in
re-enters you and crosses you over
the sleep of the living and the dead

MOVING AROUND

Tour

The rumor among the houseboat locals
was that the old volcano was waking up mad
and its snorts were tossing tourists from canoes
— the ones who try to lick the moon off the water —
but the tourists claimed the cove was full of mines.
Boats were outlawed and soon there were too many fish
for the tourists to enjoy swimming,
so to lure the rush into huge nets
the resort owners dribbled garbage into the cove
and flattered their guests into doing fancy casting
from the balconies and the cocktail veranda.

Sharks tailed in after the fish,
then rolled in shallow for the garbage
and shadowed the wading area.
The resort owners led a posse to the boats
and chased the sharks around the cove,
shooting at them and now and then
at one another just for fun and also
to keep down the drinking and dozing in the boats
until the mines went up, toppling all the resorts,
and that is why this lovely seaside village
is not included on this year's tour. However,
our bus makes a rest stop on the corniche boulevard
where they still sell last year's postcards.

I First Practiced
Picking Up Small Things

I first practiced picking up small things
with my toes. Then I hung from trees
and in a couple of weeks I got good
at looking around upside down.
Headstands at home helped. I worked
hard too on the soft drop to ground,
then added coming up into a four-legged
shuffle, and on up into a hunched run.
Next I mastered the spin-around bellow.
I was ready to leave the backyard.
I took to the fields and let fly
with swoopers. These I had practiced
nights in my room. You swing your arms
and wind them so that your shoulders
roll. This adds a lope to your run.
I go into a swooper after a soft
drop from a tree and up through
a four-legged shuffle to my hunched
run. The dogs weren't my idea
and that's when the neighbors
said they were going to lasso me,
hobble me in a corral, but I knew
they were just making fun because
there aren't any corrals around.
I was excited and then I realized
cars are a lot older and wilder
than we think. Perhaps we tamed them
too much. Anyway I want to emancipate
cars. A big idea and since you all
have one I thought I should ask you
first. I'm serious or I wouldn't
come here to our town meeting.

Bridgeport

OK I'll tell you what I like, really like
about the old days in this city. Sunsets.
That's right. Sunsets. So now the air gets
slimy as the factory smoke and all the grit

in the wind, you have to hunch to walk.
So we go out back, we sit out back,
me and Ray and Fuzzy, and watch
those colors rise, with a couple of sixpacks,

and watch them slide. We love to pick
the best second of the sunset and drink
to each best second. Then we'd holler,
that was a real skyblazer!

Sure, just another sunset and a sixpack,
but when you whoop the sky up like that
you can go half out of your head
and holler, hey Ray, hey Fuzzy, look,

the sky's all over you bastards
wherever you are, and I got a cold one here
that says keep swigging the sunset
because you haven't left me yet.

Bargain

I got 2 marriages 1 wife 1 mother
2 stepchildren 1 secretary 1 job
2 sons 2 houses 3 cars 1 daughter
1 school board 1 civic post 3 clubs
3 bank accounts 1 dog 1 boat 9 credit
cards 3 charities and the 4th tax bracket.

That gives me a total of 42. That means,
Arthur, you're 1st with 58. I buy
your martinis for a month on this train.
Toby, your 39 is 3rd. You throw in
3 days of your vacation and drive
a cab, working out of the town station.

Bruce, your 37 makes you last man.
You go to an island for a week, alone,
doing nothing. When you return
you can't tell anyone anything.

Truck

With women he felt like a truck,
the one he drove, standard shift,
hammered out fenders, the racket starting up,
heaves of turning over, then lumbering
hard off the steering wheel big as a barrel.

The women who liked him liked him like that.
The one who got him said, you love the drive,
say you do, but hate the echo when you sleep.
It drowns like the whistle of a train.
You've got to come back up,
jump the truck gone mad, that drives itself,
and grab the wheel, take it home, take it home.

American Hero:
A Poem Made Into a Movie

Silhouetted on a ledge, the grand beast known
in local legend as the Vanilla Gorilla! My posse
tumbles like dominoes. I take my fiberglass bow,
lay an arrow in, and vissst! — my arrow snips
him off, punctures his little ear so bulbous red
it looks inside out. He goes dummy on the ledge,
tips over. People want hair, clumps of it, parades,
a national holiday. Cubs, Brownies, Legionnaires,
and Miss American Aphrodite sipping warm milk
with nuns and the DAR, and girls with skin
like bubble gum, dancing the squid, the tongue,
the pneumatic drill. I'm led to a reviewing stand
where a retired WAC called Sizzles proclaims me
"Hero!" and a bear of a jukebox rolls to my chest
swelling. My heartbeat is recorded for the country.

I run for the woods, hug a tree. Something gives.
I want to be a crowd. My feet feel like galoshes.
There's Miss American Aphrodite! She's the girl
next door, girl with parents, girl with other guy.
She stares at her drink. Her ice is melting.
I feel as big as a ranch. She's coming up,
I hear her bubbling. Her face is a swimming pool.
I want to be a helicopter, hover over her, dangle
my arms to her. We go for a spin, run every light
and go the wrong way up a one-way. Faster,
faster. Water running down a sink. Grab
for the soap. Save the soap. Forget the soap.
We hit the drain with the sound of a kiss.

Chicago

He asked the waitress if she liked it here
and would she like to go with him to Chicago.
No she said. He drove on, toward Chicago,

stopping at diners, until he found another
lovely waitress. Miss, would you like to go
to Chicago with me? She said no.

Driving, he worked on a different opener.
He asked the next lovely waitress if she
wanted to take a drive around town. No

she replied. He drove. He stopped for coffee.
The waitress was lovely. He had to ask,
How about a walk in the park, a nice break?

No she said. Why not? before
he thought. You really want to know?
See this town, it stinks! Like all the other
podunks. All I want to do is go to Chicago.

Moon Gliding

Woody Creek Canyon, Colorado

A raft down the river in the moon,
moon gliding, that's what we do
when the moon climbs the bank trees
and takes the river. The raft
goes in cold, slick, and slow off
from shore until the moon quickens
on the current. Banks, trees sink
back and blur. Water rollicks
in shallow rock beds. White water
is fast, but moon water is slippery.
Glide, glide. Lifts of light tell
of boulders underwater, and over
smooth exposed stones water slides
so thin the moon goes right inside.

Universe of Kansas

I'm stranded hitching on a Kansas highway so flat if you walk you wonder if you're going. Land is a plate for air. If a car appears there's enough time to go blind. I'll evaporate first. Here comes a duster twirling along the ground. If I knew he was friendly I'd hug him. Duster, lift me out of here. Let's go play marbles with the stars. Let's yank the wrapper off the world. We'll go inside where the light is crazy bright and the air is good enough to lick. We'll be silly putty, a blue ball, a yellow yo-yo, a kite string, up into dawn and gong!

A blur trickles onto the horizon. A car, a real one! I tingle and blink. My spine is a harp, I'm played wildly. The car grows. How do I look? Must think out my skin. Look marooned. My legs are hull ribs. Come alongside, look into my porthole heart. Please start slowing down. Look, no silly smile, no billboard fake. An easy smile. You're coming so fast. My thumb, my thumb. Lean out a bit. Part of things. Having fun. Surprise. Over here. Here I am. You see me now. What a nice backseat you must have. I read maps I drive I am.

I won't wave. Just sway. You're onto me. Please stop. I don't wave. Your grill glistens, sizzles. Toes crunch. Don't wave. I wave, I wave yes wildly!

Dodo Birds

The lug shakes himself awake like a duck,
this eyewash who hit the party as if he just
got in from both coasts. His wife who talks

to feel her quiver lips move, tiptoes around
every guy here, then passes out with her hand
in the ashtray and a shag of hair cupped

over her left breast. It ends on the way down
around the icebox, something about bushes too
near the drive. Shadows shadows. They can't

drive, I can't sleep. That's fate and fried
eggs, coffee, house apologies and a tall shot
to get me home to hate, better each night,

what I've done and haven't,
like the next day, not me up for me again,
lugging my bed slab of a body to the sink.

O feel the hulk blood up, the whole rubber
tree frame flapping again, with step so sure
it goes where the eye sights down a pantleg.
If anyone asks at work, I'm a house of hair.

Lip's Lounge

They answer the phone there Lips
and lean on it. Where the tongue
goes to curl the L, I don't know,
but the i is long enough to ride
and the s rolling the p enacts
the word rippling the silence
it reverberates into. My stomach
decides, whatever doesn't have
lips wants them. Even a tongue
wants another tongue all its own.
Mine, alone in the mouth, wants
out. Lips says the bartender to
the phone and my tongue comes
out, hangs out of bed. I get
it back in, I use my hand, then
set my legs off across the room.
I like how they lip along,
how they lean in together on
the pool table and a bank shot
kissed just so the slow roll
slits the pocket clean. I'm
ready now to take the calls,
be the man who does the word.
I want the word. I practice,
curl my legs around the table
legs, inhale, lay the words in
air to air. Someday the word
will come without a sound.

King Tongue

Every burger, fry, and onion ring is his delight
to pop, breath held, down the stomach he loves
to listen to chortle and disgorge accordingly.
His T shirt boasts the Golden Arches spanning
every other symbol he has consumed within.

Underneath he's woven for his paunch rippling
*KING TONGUE DECLARES OPEN SEASON
ON FAST FOOD* and on another
THE ABSOLUTE MOUTH HAS ARRIVED,
and through the mustard-relish whirl burbling
his lips he slurs: every fast food joint
is just a lot of Army surplus to Green Fang.

He pilgrims to the desert town of Dinosaur
where the jolly pink plaster brontosaurus
named Buckaroo sits astride the fast food
dream of the world; he taps a toenail,
it pops up, and he is into upholstered pipes
lined with onion rings thick as redwoods and
knee-high chicken liver icecream toadstools.

Then the big funnel, the rushing of mustard,
and the raised silver plate with the sign
*THIS SANDWICH WILL BE FIRED INTO SPACE.
ENTER AT YOUR OWN RISK. ONLY HE WHO EATS
HIS WAY OUT WON'T JOIN THE ORGANIC FUELS.*

Our man neither reads nor counts the signatures
but steps in sampling. The authorities announce
that he is vanquished like the other sillies,
but under the high moon shadows of Buckaroo
you hear whispered rumor of a nibbling
that softens to a lick, then a pause
so silent you can feel the sigh,
the tongue doing a slow oval of the lips, then
breath rising, holding — ah — pure delight!

A Night and Morning First Time Drive to Portland

80N rises from Idaho into Oregon until,
shy of Pendleton, the night opens
across an old ocean floor and my lights dive turns
so deep they have cut escape ramps
for trucks that lose it heaving down.
And they only call this Cabbage Hill.

I unwind from Cabbage Hill onto a dry plain,
the air filling with the light before dawn.
I roll down my window, smell the Columbia River
coming down from the North, and meet her
after breakfast, bending west
to the Pacific. My rearview mirror flickers,
bursts white. Light strikes the river
like love enough for an army.

Above the gorge cliffs, something that looks like
kin to the sun — Mt. Hood! Half the cone
is snow in August. Snow over Columbia blue,
barges frisking the whitecaps,
snow over tan grasses waving the river to the road,
snow over cliff green that could put my car to sleep.
What a mountain! I bet it comes out in Portland
as you're walking down a street.

Hands

My hands can't forget you being here.
They fiddle. I rub them above my eyes,
crinkle the skin down over and close
my eyes deeper on you moving away.
Where are you thinking of now?
You have so many places you could be
here, and take my hands again as if
you were taking them with you
and swing them as if they could fly.
You said I looked good. What did I say?
My hands, they fiddle and grind.
When will I be like you, so easily here,
saying you dropped in and will again?
Then I can let you go easily and
my hands can open in a deep breath.

Bottoming Out

Driving at night and my lights go out
at sixty. I'm wired wide-eyed
yelling inside miles away that won't
be here. I'm here, be here, the car's blind!
The brake? No, I'd be piled from behind,

Their lights liquid in the back window.
The lights in front I freeze on. The dark
must have a zipper. No, I'm doing a gawk
skin and bone right out to zero.
Get off the road! Gun it, now slow, slow,

And stop. Believe ground. The dead
eyes, kick them into the dashboard.
Kick the holes. Carlights swish over like
huge slow bullets. I lift my hands
into them. Hands want to cleat bark.

I rush a tree, chip off bark.
It tastes like hair rolled for days
and glued. I want to pry myself open,
lift the spine out whole, pull it back
like a bow, set my head in,
and fire my head away.

The Lady with the Laughing Gas Lover

He liked her especially because she got him laughing
gas from the dentist she worked for. She said
she wouldn't, but she wanted to surprise him. She did.
The dentist liked her especially because she asked
every time and was loyal to this jerk of a guy.
She liked the dentist especially because he didn't ask
weird things of her or yell about her wanting to ask
every time, which hurt, or sail off goofed on the gas.

Then one day the dentist got laughing so hard
she figured he was on the gas. He was embarrassed
and when he realized what she must be thinking,
he sputtered, "No, I'm not, honest!" She was confused
because she still wanted to see if any was missing.
He gabbed about how he hadn't laughed like this in years.
"Years!" lofting his arms, and giggled. She wanted to
hug him, she liked him so. She cried because he was nice
and what a jerk she was in love with.

And especially because she wanted to get him all
the gas he wanted and hated his laughing gas jags.
Right there, the dentist could have kissed her,
loved her joyously, but asked "What's wrong?"
and they became especially polite to one another.

So when she came home after an especially polite
day and her lover started in about how nice
the dentist is and how nice she is for keeping him
in the gas, which he loves, stressing the point
so that she wouldn't think he was selling the stuff,
she began to cry, which surprised him, worried him,
angered him. Then she laughed. "What's so funny?"
"Oh nothing," she replied, "I wish I had some gas
for you." "I don't need any gas!" he bellowed.
"Good," she said and politely tried to relax him.

Demolition of Grand Central Station

And buses, they should go deep like whales,
surface far off, blow, sun and roll,
far from this construction site, here on this day
of demolition, when the crane line swings,
when the arc of the ball includes the wall.

I am going to the lower level to my train,
down the escalator and clacking stairs,
across to the tunnel and ramp to my platform,
down to face people across the ditch of tracks,
waiting for another train. Their platform fills,
their train pulls in, cuts them away.

They come back on in the carlights of their train.
Windows frame the walking flow waist high.
Their walking seems to move the train.
My days of watching store windows pass me on,
of boarding a bus someday and asking the driver
the name of a place that everyone cheers.